FEDER

NATHANAËL

FEDER

a scenario

NIGHTBOAT
BOOKS

NEW YORK

OR

.
.
.
.
.
.
.

"THE LIVING THEMSELVES"

137. We could imagine a glass through which black looked like black, white like white, and all the other colours appeared as shades of grey; so that seen through it everything appears as though in a photograph. // But why should I call that "white glass"?

Ludwig Wittgenstein

History is what hurts,

Fredric Jameson

An obsolescent acception of obsolescence:

The almost complete effacement of a marking on a bird's plumage, an animal's coat, etc.

O.E.D.

PRINCIPLES OF ENDAMAGEMENT

To my own Ludwig, who first introduced me to Feder — *für mein abendes N.*

It goes without saying.

Between the glass and the Masonite is a layer of air in which are suspended a small number of paper tickets of varying thicknesses and dimensions. The principle of their assemblage is unfounded. Say they span a period of time extending from March to September of a given year. A time without narration. They are held in place by the air itself and the metal clips pressing the glass to the board. Periodically, the tickets adjust their position, upheld against the temptations proffered by gravity. There is no protest. No conversation is recorded under the concrete awning at a particularly windy junction. Nor is there evidence of restraint, touch, or trembling. The city is not accounted for, nor the bodies nearing one another. What is certain, though, is that this record of occasions is already a record of obsolescence. Perhaps because of the heat from the incandescent bulb in the Machine Age gooseneck lamp on the wooden table where the tickets sit collected before being pushed into the frame. Perhaps because of the oils from the fingers that held them before setting them there, uninked, blanched. Whatever was said went unrecorded. Whatever was intended was unsaid. Whatever was meant was reabsorbed into the air that stayed caught behind the glass.

I'm looking now.

I'm looking right at the thing. When I pick it up to read it, I realize I can't read any more than I can speak. So I look again. If I were to repeat myself, I might find that there is a subjective fault in the place of the repetition of me.

I

ACCIDENT

It is in the fold between these two impossibilities — the imminent obliteration of the witness, the certain unrepresentability of the testimony — that the photographic image suddenly appeared.

Georges Didi-Huberman

Muß er?

Feder climbs the brief stair. He climbs the brief stair always up. The one stair and the next indistinguishable. There is the foot on the stair. Or he might say that the foot resorts to the stair. It is the north emergency stair, each day the same. So he does not count them. Up or down, he does not count. Today Feder finds an insect on the stair in the usual place. It lies upturned with its feet in the air. He is reassured by the placement of the insect. He cannot recall a time when the insect was not there. He scarcely notices it as he pulls the heavy metal door and disappears into the corridor.

There are rows and stacks. And windows occasionally. The room is divided into squares of shadow and light. A dark light nonetheless. A ceilinged room and underfoot a floor. It is no point making an assumption about the constitutive elements of the room nor attempting to ascertain its dimensions. Nothing of the room is different today compared to yesterday. No one sees it empty or fill.

There is a flicker. Someone has forgotten to replace the seal.

A hand pushes aside a small mound of dirt. The insect is dropped onto its back and covered over with care.

Among the rows and stacks one might imagine a line of smoke and a slow, undeliberate asphyxiation. It is not remarkable. A dull knocking perhaps. An iron grate at another moment in history.

These are not the counted bodies. There is nothing left to be counted. Not because of a lack of objects. Simply the system of numbers upon which they had hitherto relied had fallen into disuse.

In the time before there were many accusations. There were many trials. The people stood and they sat. The transcripts are indicative of negation. Several untranslated languages have accounted for this. The substitutive passages maintain a strong indication of hopefulness.

It is Feder's job to light the fires.

It had a name.

In the fields cut up into city blocks the name was pronounced many times. Sometimes shouted. No one doubted the force of the name. And so it was repeated often. The water was brought to a very high temperature according to custom and the people moved around on their knees. In the moments when the structure was overturned, the people appeared to be suspended from a sky of concrete.

The body at the foot of the stair shows no evidence of having fallen. The head is at an awkward angle. Since the stair is seldom employed, the body is not remarked upon.

In the small adjacent garden the fountain is being drained. The gate is pulled shut and the low wall is worn. Periodically the stones are removed, brushed off and replaced in the same order in which they were initially assembled. There is no record of the wall having been built and the city ordinance requiring that it be taken down and rebuilt at regular intervals has been misplaced. The task as it is outlined requires that each stone resume its initial placement. This applies to chipped or cracked stones as well. The time allotted to the habitual disassembly and immediate reconstruction of the wall is insufficient. Reports have been filed in protest with little success. The workers are required to report to the captain of the work site in advance of the assignment of their duty.

Even if someone had seen the body land there, none would have been able to identify it as the body of a person. Whether it had fallen from a great height or collapsed in the exact place where it happened to be standing, the fall had exerted a great strain on the features of the face. Why assume a misdeed? If the body had indeed been carrying something, the something was gone. The registry of missing persons will not be consulted. Nor will the stolen effects be searched for and retrieved.

But the body is lying face down.

This is not unusual in coastal cities and border towns where jurisdictions are under much dispute. It will not matter that the body may have come from somewhere. The thread is snapped. The method of the body's disposal is yet to be determined. This case resembles so many others of its kind and requires caution and tact.

Sir?

Is it sleeping?

Feder had not considered the possibility of this particular outcome any more than another. His emotion was as indisputable as it was irrelevant.

To begin with, there was nothing to forgive. Had the event been recorded, there would have been a consensus as to its lack of consequence. Certainly, as it was, it had been thoroughly exhausted. The materials in question were gathered pell-mell in a shut room. Marble walls and green terra-cotta. A brass mail chute in the plaster and engraved wood mouldings along the ceilings and floors. If there was a resonance, it was purely imaginary and what was retained of it was its depletion.

Nothing stood in its way.

The electrical room could be heard setting itself in motion.

Feder was not unaware of the removal of the weight-bearing walls but it had not seemed important to report it. The dispersal of objects over surfaces belied the need for acute observation. And if it happened that an accident did present itself, there would be time indeed to attend to it with the appropriately accented gesticulations. He scarcely knew the sound of his own voice, and this was of no concern to him. It did, however, make him a rather unreliable witness.

At the centre of the city a thronging crowd converges beneath banners and cries. It emerges from a tunnel of obelisks and tracks, risen and pronged.

A body scarcely visible runs from the camera. One imagines it victorious in flight, over the hill and into oblivion. Or else ligatured to a horizon of hope. A voice trails after it, carried on the sound of streets converging at a monument. But no. The sound is an imagining as well. Wrenched from a spinning reel.

A torn cloth striking the air.

Arms raised: a supplicant proviso.

All these years! All these years!

By the way, in what way is it wrong for a picture?

Ludwig Wittgenstein

In the funnel created by the courtyard, the windows are deprived of their function. No light enters by them and no rain strikes them in the faintest of mists or the most violent of downpours. It is an uncalculated consequence of design. A falsehood upholding the real. The combination of the absence of light and the absence of remarkable inclemency results in an unverifiable state of turbulence.

If one donned an overcoat before exiting the building, it was out of sheer despair, for there was no indication, ever, of its purposefulness.

The eyes of the wearers grow dim.

They are in a state of desuetude. The tactic aspirations of this architecture are misleading. In a historical sense, their anteriority has been squandered on a sense of immediacy that is no longer readily available.

Feder sets the mechanisms to work. He is very much to blame.

The questions take the form of accusations. Whether they are pronounced by a single mouth or several is not made clear in the transcripts since the lines all run into one another. 'Did you or did you not' is struck out several times.

The conclusions rely on the notion of super-cession to reduce the likelihood of an appeal. Person-hood is revoked according to the usual procedures.

It is worth noting that the names of those present are whited out.

What is the measure of your worth?

What made you think you would go unnoticed?

Did you think at all?

Did you express disappointment? Surprise?

The meeting takes place in a depressed, reinforced chamber, in the congested epicentre of a large North American city.

Was anybody hurt?

For the sake of expediency, Feder washes his hands in a small basin near the main corridor. He rarely, if ever, looks up.

The articles are arranged sequentially. It is his task to number them. If he makes an error, a wooden mallet strikes him several times on the back.

Though the building is equipped with the most advanced technologies, the clock chimes according to ancient tradition.

Oft he

: a beat repeated untiringly in the same time represents the faithful copy of a rhythmic atom (but an antique metre is already a rhythmic molecule repeating itself). However, small variations in the time produce an internal vivacity of the rhythm without weakening the fundamental period. Greater and more complex variations of the fundamental period create a disfigurement, a negation of the fundamental period that could lead to its immediate unrecognizability.

Feder takes this to mean that music has the same basic characteristics as a bombardment. Meticulously, he divests himself of any and all devices in his possession that may enliven the persistence of this memory. These include a tattered copy of Lucretius's *De Rerum Natura*, a contemporary *Bratsche*, only slightly damaged, and an intact gramophone from the set of *Brighton Rock*.

Feder's research leads him to confound music and militarism. On his daily ascent up the north stairwell, he acquires a strong aversion to the sound of his own footsteps. He understands these to be imitative of his heart and as he acquires this understanding the blood pours steadily from his ears.

The war department has meanwhile found a way to send untraceable radioactive particulate into skin. Its contaminative effects produce astonishing instances of human conflagration. The inventors of this technology congratulate themselves on the isolating quality of the weapon, which is considered mild in light of the absence of a contagion. Feder does not dream of this. In his sleep he extracts his own eyes and pushes them off the windowsill.

But who is spreading these rumours? He is watching a film again. Besides the obvious temporal ramifications of the form, it must be noted that the mind, contrary to a commonly held belief, only resembles the cinema insofar as it is a concatenation of syncopes. Méliès's stop-trick was no surprise to the senses, but how can one be sure of this?

We will try again.

The non sequitur's obvious rival is historical continuity. Syntactically, the articulation of this principle of discord takes the form of an insistent refutation of existence (ontology) and the resistance, in all of its aspects, of self-referentiality (the script).

In the absence of a self, there is neither anteriority nor interiority.

Architecturally, this is made manifest by various means, most persistently through the use of one-way mirrors. The coincidence of reflectivity and transparency provokes an unresolvable somatic contradiction which is most apparent at a building's flexion. Locating it is another problem altogether, since it has no discernible geography.

Feder is really in for it.

Judgement at Language

The split screen proffers duplicate instances of misarticulation. The interview is recorded over several days and dubbed always with a delay. There is one existing transcript only. It is a transcript, not of the interview itself, but of the interview recast with the overlay of the interpreter's voice. When the voice of the artist is heard, it is included in the transcript, and interrupted with ellipses before being translated into a single recuperative language: suggestive of what has been said and crossed out by the interpreter for the sake of intelligibility.

It is clear from the above that the artist has no actual voice.

The conversation between Errera and Arendt is a lost conversation. Evidently lost in an effort of translation. What subsists of their language is ushered into the transcript as artefact. That is, its temporality is belated. It is the extant trace of a thing mediated by its own mortification. In this respect, the transcript, a record of a translation, with words, sometimes passages, replaced by a series of X's due to indecipherability, draws out the intransigent relationship between translation and censure:

.... if only they would say it, they are afraid, they are afraid to be afraid ....

If Feder.

But the conditional does not apply to Feder. When he walks he walks up. And the corridors he borrows as his footpaths anticipate nothing of his movement. His traversals are not conjurings of other traversals. Nor do they manifest as reversals. They do as they undo, just as they undo as they do not, while the small unforgotten insect deteriorates. By now its articulations are indistinguishable from the dirt into which they have been thrust. They do not fossilize. Nor can Feder be said to be a fossil. He is very much alive. To be alive is to be alive with the dust as it is accentuated by the light that hovers in the atmosphere. He takes no notice of it, however. It is not in his purview to do so. If he were to look up, he might be astonished by what he saw. But his attention draws him to the immediate present with its plane surfaces and brief, uncalculated distances. They are uncalculated because they are obvious. Much in the way Feder's emotion need not be mentioned, ever. If he has any antecedents, they have been removed either by force or by circumstance. The same may be said for Feder's interiority. The happy consequence of these deliberate omissions is that he may grant his full attention to the tasks to which he has been duly designated. Feder's jurisdiction is only limited by his line of vision. Certainly, he has not attended to the scrolls in some time, but the aperture is securely fastened shut, thus reducing the likelihood of theft or water damage. The oxidation of the hinges has been seen to. For now he must resort to thinking. If he does not do so, then his fist may resort to the tabletop or knock a lamp to the floor. But this is not the Feder we had in mind. Our Feder is tranquil.

It weeps from the left side of the face only. One eye weeps and the other remains dry. Many have stood before it and admired the inconsistency. The name Janus has been pronounced in earnest and much surmising as to its origin has occupied the minds of many, each in private, for none of it is spoken as such. There it stands, in isolate silence, the left eye running rivulets down a stone cheek.

Is it stone, really?

Two faces in one. Or else two halves of two separate faces, combined to produce such subtle grotesquerie. It needn't matter. If the hands are to be praised then so are the eyes to be contrived. It is a clouded vision that claims clarity. And a right mind that seeks unjustly to correct a deformity. If it is a deformity of the good sense of seeing, it is a deformity also of a similar refusal. A stone square, a malady of time, a frailty of the mind that imagines such things. But what is this 'it' exactly? What exactitude is summoned in the absence of a reasonable argument? Is there a body with the face? Is there even a face? Or is all of it invented for the sake of not going mad with it? A madness surely that could easily be explained by temperament or doctrine. Inside the buildings, it is quite agreed upon that there is no such thing. But none have yet determined what buildings are meant, nor whether this side faces outward or not. And what a building is, my friend, is very unattributable to such reasonings. I was quite certain that each was a fool with his conjecture. But this is a conjecture of my own and a sure sign of foolishness. Up and up. And so it went. The eye is not glass nor stone as far as I can tell, but none can be bothered to examine it. The fear is that it will announce an imponderable future sunken into a revolted past and there will the mind go with it. That is the kind of nonsense one encounters in storybooks and wars the likes of which we have amply seen. So the eye cries and cries and the ground on this side of the face has already given way some.

It has quite lost its measure.

At the centre of a provincial city in an insignificant country of Western Europe, a tram cable becomes detached from the nexus of wires overhead and falls without warning into a busy intersection at midday. By the time the tram has moved through the intersection and the sound of clanging chains has alerted somnolent ears to the fact of the event, the man is already re-enacting the moment at which the cable failed to strike him, shattering instead the glass wall indicating the parochial stairs down into an equally parochial Metropolitan. The man is pointing at the wall. This is not a city for sentimentality. Nor are the people in the street particularly alerted to the significance of this otherwise innocuous incident (innocuous because no one was objectively harmed by the cable, a thickly braided length of wire equivalent to the distance between sidewalks, which is to say exceeding the length of an exceedingly long person). The incident occurred as anticipated, between the florist's and the tailor's — a Japanese ivy and a thick sewing needle. It claimed the life of a single foreigner not present at the event and drew its impetus from either one of the world wars. The pigeons in the square with their paper wings ascended. They heard the shot just as the foreigner did, before being struck by it. None of this is of course verifiable in the empirical sense, the evidence having been ushered into the atmosphere by a series of timely circumstances — each visible to the naked eye.

Feder, what have you to say for yourself?

The monolithic relics strewn across four thousand kilometres of coastline are ill-disposed toward the elements. We come down for the aweless pillage.

I am well aware that most images are of no consequence.

Georges Didi-Huberman

The following are classifications of fingerprint patterns proposed in a Royal Institution paper in 1888, and in a series of books published respectively in 1892, 1893, and 1895 and titled *Fingerprints, Decipherment of Blurred Finger Prints*, and *Fingerprint Directories* by Francis Galton:

1: *plain arch*, 2: *tented arch*, 3: *simple loop*, 4: *central pocket loop*, 5: *double loop*, 6: *lateral pocket loop*, 7: *plain whorl*, and 8: *accidental*.

The latter is of particular interest.

The search had been underway for several days. The various factions had been alerted as to the disappearance of a key member. The following weeks demanded discursive stasis. If 'several days' was a suitable referent, 'years and years' was not. The measurement of time, the allowable periodicity for the fantasy of the search did not exceed seventy-two hours, such that the event of the disappearance tolerated only its renewal, rejecting its reiteration. The operation was a successful exercise in amnesic reformulation. Neither short- nor long-term memory sufficed as methods of obliterative calculation. The hermeticism of the architecture saw to it that not even a shadow would graze the interior walls. The lighting, designed to avoid such visual faults imitated the lighting methodologies applied to public thoroughfares. If a sound were to enter from the outside, it was immediately corrected. Beyond the city limits, the immediate insurgency of sound was notable. Barriers were erected to control this effect.

The material result of these modifications is anachronistic. Formerly speaking — it is perhaps the only possible mode of composition in this instance — the event such as it is surmised and objected to takes place in a prior mode. At times, it is true,

Feder opens one of the doors to which he is assigned onto a selection of catalogues, each pertaining to a precise activity or form. Their belated necessity is in his handling of them. If the concordance were in the form and its record, the strain on his neurological constitution would be intolerable. Many times throughout the day he wipes his brow. This is to avert perspiration or perplexity, not to address it as a fact of his own body's encounter with the world. Besides, there is no evidence to corroborate such a relation.

The first catalogue contains a series of photographs evidencing the eugenic experimentations of Francis Galton. Feder blinks several times and wipes his hands back and forth along his thighs. The photographs are composites. Their intent is to expose moral defects, among criminals or patients with tuberculosis for example, to arrive at the type of the criminal through the superimposition of traits. The same procedure may be applied to the faces of humans exhibiting qualities ascribed to genius. A single photographic plate provides the surface for multiple faces.

The first task is to lift prints from the paper. The following summary is provided in the preliminary notes:

A murder.
A riot.
A garden.
A mechanism.
An archive.
An interrogation.
A camera.
A slow and intolerable music.

For a moment, Feder believes he is being watched. It is a game he likes to play with himself.

On his way out, he is careful to shake the dust from his epaulettes.

The shape of it is indisputably sad. The ascribed geometric values serve to regulate the emotion of it. In the improvised morgues, for example, the annunciatory subservience of the gymnasium to the morbid figures predicts the designation of further public spaces to the compilation of death counts. The recorded surveys of unidentified corpses under various dictatorships yield a similar problem of nomination. In this parlance, row 29, for example, functions semantically in a way not dissimilar to a mass grave. The heavy rains wash the bodies onto the street. The resulting pandemonium indicates a need to bury the dead above ground. In each instance, casts are made of the extant faces and subsequently smashed in the public squares. This is to ensure the eradication of an exact nomenclature and to limit the period allocated to mourning.

What has any of this got to do with architecture? Feder adjusts the controls and limits the passage of light.

If I am my own shadow.

Feder begins this thought and suspends it. Such conjecture is unequivocally discouraged. If he stopped to count the stories stacked beneath his desk, he would not then be able to recuse the fact of the downwardness of the back stair. His gaze is level. The hairs on the back of his neck lie flat.

For God's sake, man, leave it alone.

We are eminent, eminent. In the still unspoken night, we speak toward speaking.

Did Leonardo really cut the bodies open?

In the planted gardens, the roots burrow down. There is no light and so they burrow more deeply and lift the edifices from the ground, wrapping themselves around the support beams and striking at the glass. The sound of the night is that shattering.

Each body is relieved very deftly of the clavicle. The breathing continues uninterrupted as the fragile bone snaps.

A bird in the window.

Ghastly.

First one, and then another.

None of these phenomena need be unreasoned.

Hand me that shovel.

The real begs its own question. It will not be settled like this, without proper apprehension.

But Sir, why have you called us here, and at such an hour?

The window is a permissive medium for a thickening obscurity. There is no succour at this hour of the night. The persistent rain drives the glass pane deeper into the casement. The subsequent appearance of an untendered image is considered rash and models a kind of unvisible skin. The real, in this instance, is ceremoniously held back.

Feder does not force his way. There is no need for it. The armature does not cede, though there are slight internal rupturings. What is most apparent becomes less so as the day lifts its guise. That is, assuming such a differentiation. The first deliveries arrive well after Feder's installment at his desk and the progressive streaks of light stripping the space of its density. He might describe his own head as a strobe under these effects, but is engrossed in several small objects that have escaped supervisory description. The vertical inclination of the project is altogether haphazard. At another geographical location, a more expansive complex might be alluded to, then possibly implemented. For the moment, it remains pure conjecture, and is, as a result, unfathomable. These are the petty machinations of repetitive entry and do nothing to advance operations. The most urgent concern is of course the distribution of privations. A vertical alignment of rectangular recesses in the wall opens and shuts its iron traps. A hollow knocking resounds. Thereupon several bodies are seen to be falling from high windows. Each is disposed of immediately, indicating to a searching populace the futility of subsequent questionings. It remains unclear, however, whether the seabed can accommodate such populations, and what effect such additions to the oceanic flora will have on the tides.

None at all.

Feder loosens his collar. A vein throbs persistently at his temple. A bead of sweat forms over one eye. His right leg twitches under the wooden boards of his desk. The lights flicker and illumine as before. These minor irregularities evidence looming beleaguerment though these terms are not those which will be employed.

The hostilities are imaginatively orchestrated to insinuate themselves into the captive bodies which will then seek their own destruction. The surrounding area is blockaded, though to ill effect. The biologic proposal favours internal somatic combustion. There is no need to propel oneself from a window ledge. Given enough time, the body will dispose of itself. What is unpredictable is the intensity of the cry.

Further sighs emerge from the mouths of the workers. Feder is just one such artisan. Though his responsibilities are far more elaborate.

Nostalgia is, in this instance, sheer wantonness. To die willingly, or as a matter of course.

Do you know Argentina?

Small mechanical errors register systemic disquiet without much warning. The signals, though imperceptibly altered, continue to guide the movement as priorly ordained. The advantage over such programming is that it need only periodic revision. If a glitch should introduce itself between revisions, then it will have the benefit of a brief hiatus within which to wreak a limited amount of havoc. Enough to be perceivable upon the next revision. If, however, its subterfuge is sufficiently clever as to pass unnoticed, then it will be able to insinuate itself into the very functioning of the mechanism.

The crowd that gathers around the body is quickly dispersed. It is days now, perhaps weeks, since it has been lying there, at the foot of the stair. Because it gives no immediate evidence of decay, the body is assumed to be that of a sleeping person, and thus an inconvenience to occasional foot traffic. Because, however, its position is so idiosyncratic, it is left undisturbed in its slumber. Under the blanket a fine line of blood has trickled its way into the public square. Because of the ambient temperatures, no notice is given to this particular sign, and so the body is granted its silent demise.

The fist of history is mighty that will fall upon the fool who looked the other way.

But surely we are looking, are we not? Straight into the mouth of it. With its rotten teeth and foul breath and nicotine stains. The stench concealed by the rank of the edifice itself. Does it wreak of death? Perhaps it is we who stink. We are the ones, after all, who had it built.

Must we pity the Pharaohs their Egypt?

I saw her, Sir, it was I. In the exact place where she fell.

Feder, help us move this cabinet, will you?

The chocolatiers are first rate. They are the great purveyors of the everlasting century. It could just as easily have been the furriers. The great institutions lined their walls with fur the way they line their innards with chocolate, fantastical though it may seem. It was an acquired taste of decadence. A new expressionism. Everything askew and finely linened. This was necessary in order to accommodate the assassinations. These were a hallmark of advancement, and attested to the intransigency of an acquired disgrace.

Numbers are so fickle. Eleven million. Thirty thousand. Eight hundred thousand. Thirty-four.

What Feder doesn't understand is how it is the mail is so late. He has been poring over the same document for several hours now. Though time does sometimes stand still for him, the mail always arrives on schedule. Now this too will have to be questioned.

Without warning, Feder looks across the room. It is neither as big as he had imagined it nor as narrow as he had become accustomed to. I am no insect, he thinks to himself, adjusting the angle of the century. He touches the edge of his chair and remembers he has not eaten in days, possibly weeks. An elevator opens on a lower floor. Shouting can be heard. He adjusts his collar.

Dust continues to gather in the corners. Tomorrow, he will attend to it.

Not far from there, a group of children has unearthed the morbid bug. One after another they pluck off its legs, scattering them like wishes.

Tomorrow is a word that had not occurred to Feder before. The whole mechanism grinds to a halt.

II

PRIGIONIERE

IMAGINATION therefore is nothing but *decaying sense*; and is found in men, and many other living Creatures, as well sleeping, as waking.

Thomas Hobbes

I saw Argentina in the body of a boy. She was struggling to be free. Her sorrow was strained and her city was solarized. She grabbed at ceilings and ornate swings and turned walls from their foundations and gathered dogs at her heels. In the event, I heard her say, repeatedly, in the event. And she entered there unbidden, and emerged unwilled. There were hands that reached toward her, and birds that filled the sky, and windows that cracked from the many wind storms and springs that circulated underground. Her clothing was outmoded and her speech was forlorn, and her emotion denied the commonplace and startled the crowd, and none listened even though she spoke aloud. For every street lamp a grenade was launched. For every shattered eardrum an abandoned outpost. The debris floated on the seas and the seas floated on the ash and the ships sank the onlookers and there were sparrows with gulls and blackbirds with geese and one after another the stones fell and the bodies became exposed and the names fell into desuetude. I touched her name and the letters fell away, and what I was left with was ilié. And this was given to the boy, though not by me nor by her directly. They coupled at a centre, and there she struggled and he as well, holding his stomach and she pushing against his organs, pulling oranges from trees and whispering grand avenues and plucking the boulevards of their daisies. She boarded a tram with the Jugendstil hovering above her head in gold leaf and stucco and bundles of grapes and she pulled them off their soft stems, launching them beneath the wheels of cars. Who is to say what she might claim of history or whether the boy is aware of her despair, which is by turns his own. She grasps downward and upward and the dream she dreams is filled with viscera and violent love, escalators and detention centres, conveyor belts and bones and rotten meat. The film is projected despite its mediocrity and a meeting is arranged in a by now familiar place. She rises in the way one falls and is greeted with a fervour reserved for murder or dispassion. If she dies, she dies willingly, but she is not prepared to die yet. She runs down the brightly lit halls, she crawls along the street, she eats with both hands. She wraps seas into her sleep. Her charge is unbearable, and what I see is unrecountable, were it not for her name, Argentina. Argentina, as she is lowered into the ground.

Argentina refuses to specify. She holds a series of documents in one hand, which take the form of a fan. It is hot in this country. The officials are relatively unconcerned. They will make her wait. The questions come in swift succession. None of which she evades. Simply, she refuses to specify. Name. As if a name could settle any question at all. This country is a southern country or else it is a northern country in summer. In either instance, there is a rise in the murder rate at the first of spring or hurricane season, which Argentina refers to as the tempest. But the tempest could mean any place also.

She is awaiting confirmation. She may be asked to strip herself of her clothes. It is more likely she will be made to stand like this until tomorrow, well after the ship will have left the harbour. But there are other ships, and plenty of fools, she thinks.

Does she think this?

Her mind is closed to us. She stands still for the photograph.

There is no ship. There is no sea. The airstrips by now are obsolete. So where does Argentina think she's going?

Geography, like anything else, is a kind of conviction.

Am I a likeness to the living?

A certain brutality in the mental image.

Walter Benjamin

Dov'è?

Feder sits up in bed. The smell of formol reaches his nose before his eyes are able to focus. If it is his own bed, it is careening down an elevator shaft. If it is a hospital bed, it is being driven to the morgue, and if this is the case, then it isn't a bed at all, but a gurney. What is a bed anyway? None of these options seems plausible, however, and he is quick to adjust his glasses which ought to be sitting on the bridge of his nose.

The thought of Feder waking or sleeping is incommensurable with his industrious vigil. Away from the stair and the doors on their carefully oiled hinges, Feder seems less and less amenable to the surroundings which are imputed to him. See the grocer now, handing him a bag of apples, or the dentist adjusting him in his chair. See the teacher correcting his posture as a child. A voice bellowing at him through a telephone.

No. Feder's is a world of silence. He has not been beset with the curse of a childhood nor the advent of beginnings, nor even something that might resemble a duration. Without the wherewithal of a past which may or may not be burdensome, there cannot be anything resembling a present, with its purported plenitudes or excoriations, its lavender and its languorous afternoons. Is he alive? If so, then he shall die. Is he dead? If that is the case, then surely, he will have lived. Neither seems consistent, however, with time's assiduous manipulations. Here is a man, who is no man, in a time, which is no time. And still the people fall from the windows of buildings.

If I sing, I sing false.

Here he is now, standing in the middle of a road, with dark circles under his eyes.

Tell me, how will you bring him back?

That a man could be a man. There is indifference in it. The first epoch is dismissive. And so, dismissed, we are summoned to it, battering down its door. Setting fire to ourselves to ignite the indolent sky. But who said there was a sky or remove? The doors open in two directions, I insist upon it. This is a theatre of disclosure, in which the gravest indiscretions are corrected by measurements hitherto unenforced. It was Ionesco who impressed that his plays were tragedies, all. The condition of the tragic character was its brokenness; this was its evidence of the real — its assignment of selfhood. But who would dare say I under such conditions? Surely, the imposition of character is a grave error of intention. If I put my feet up a wall, this need elucidate nothing about gravity. However, if the wall should fall...

What are you on about now?

Look here. A violaceous dust scarcely visible around the head and the hands.

The body's pigment?

Voice, I should think.

I sing of the arms of a man.

Shut up.

I am listening in, now, at the garden gate. As long as no one moves the body, we can go on like this. Stabbing at the hard earth with our forks and our fantasy. I have let a vine grow around my ankle. When the circulation is gone from my foot, I shall get up and walk.

From the gate to the foot of the stair, one must count several centuries and at least a few cities, possibly a body of water. The problem, at present, seems to be determining the direction of time. It seems split along a seam that runs forwards and backwards, stripping the land of its names and bending it toward an incredible chronology. Never mind that for now. You will have your geography yet.

There is no point going on like this. We have visited the sites of various outpourings. Our principle specimens include the hawthorn and the baobab. The first for its decorative dagger, the second for its poison, surely, but its hermaphroditism also. Our first fervour is a grey cast, like the skin's hue in any light such as might be encountered hereabout. There is only one last philosophy and it is a prelude to a noiseless symphony comprised of irreconcilable parts. To be cast as the last of the last is to bequeath oneself to a fastidious past. *Nunca Más* as a way of begging redundancy.

History, like the law, has designated as its preferred specimen the isolated incident. It is the exception that reinforces the rule of grammar or good conduct, the mad ruler who normalises the populace, the sadistic killer who exonerates the hatred in all of us. The conduit directing effluent away from the thick stacks toward a volatile river, all eyes on the tennis match.

What difference does it make whether Feder sits at a nineteenth-century oak roll-top desk or a skyscraper industrial desk constructed of gunmetal and stainless steel. Nor whether he sifts papers under a U.S. military standard issue M1 helmet or a fedora. The French for cap is *casquette*, which recalls the English casket in sound alone. We might thus arrive at an equation in language which corroborates the morbidity of thought.

In photographic terms, facial features are internal to the face. They are both what define the face, and what are indefinable in a face. In addition, they exceed what, in a face, is visible. Like Antonioni's process of latensification, whereby photographic film can, at least in conjecture, be perennially developed to disclose unseen elements in an image. Their progressive exposure to the hitherto disadvantaged eye, layer by layer, until the complete image comes into view, does not (necessarily) result in acute precision, as one might suspect, but in an eventual black mass. Surely, this is what Koudelka came upon when he left his images to macerate too long in the developer. Thus would the absolute image be black, not white. A thick amassment of detail, so intricate as to be indiscernible (Rothko's chapel paintings, for example). The surface fallen from itself, as it were; a strange luminescence. Because surely, the eye could not accommodate such a surface at its retina. It would, so to speak, come away with itself.

When the body is submitted to its exposure, only three people are present, one of whom is standing a blunt distance away, out of propriety, perhaps, or disinterest. The stair, in the meantime, has been repainted, the same metallic grey, an otherwise indiscernible alteration to the space, were it not for the residual vapours. The blanket is pulled back very briefly. A shutter flickers, the room becomes recessed, volatile creatures alight from the eaves in a scattering of wings, and dive headlong into a lake.

The face of the head assigned to the body stretched out beneath the blanket is charred. It is a face without a face, bereft of its interior surfaces. Retrieved from what oven? History will be of no use to us here.

Someone chokes into a handkerchief. Such archaisms as handkerchiefs. Surely this someone spat up on the floor. This is a modern city.

There is no call for that now.

What will you remember of this?

You there, with your head turned.

There's nothing to see Sir.

You are mistaken. There is everything to see, Sir.

The alligators take turns swimming back and forth in the tank. It doesn't occur to anyone that this is a waiting room.

I slept through a storm. I was woken by it. A shovel scraped rock near a window. There was the sound of glass gently splintering. Boots squelching through mud and waves lapping angrily. Then a dull silence and a machine starting up.

A small car races through the night. The roads are empty. No one sees the car speed along the streets. The engine revs at the stop light and bolts onto the tarmac once the signal is given. It propels itself across the glint surfaces past the suspended buildings, the unlit fields and occasional street lamps, an unheard whir all the way to the city limits, beyond the suburbs and straight into the lake. The bodies found floating some distance from there the following morning are not fished out, but allowed to wend their way into the sewers, where their decomposition will be registered in the slight changes in levels to the city water supply. The human tendency is distinctly cannibal.

No reason is given. This is the exact place where a sea dried out. The waters drained salt onto its shores, sifting its tides into unseen interiors. A perfect reversal. What is desert was once sea. What was once sea is dry land now, and strewn with the corpses of gulls, remnants of concrete piers, wooden docks and the vestiges of lighthouses, gutted. The fish died out long before.

A body propels itself now through a revolving door, spinning with the centuries. There is no memory of a sea nor of a desert, simply the certainty of Formica and iridescent linoleum, asbestos. Filth-encrusted edges. Footworn. Inscrutable.

All of this escapes Feder, who is seated at his desk as usual, in deep study. A glint of light catches his ring and saws his finger off. He jumps up as his cry is immediately swallowed into the vacuum. Red, like the sea of his obliterated memory.

How does the garden feel when the gate is drawn shut?

*Show me a man and I will show you a thousand
more like him.*

Someone threatens to defect. The cabins
have been searched, this is standard procedure, and
the scheduled departures have all been suspended.
The more enterprising resistance is taking the lower
road, but the result for them will be the same. The
occupation is well disguised and the collaborationist
intellectuals will exonerate themselves and assemble
the new executioners. But who is speaking of
execution? This is not Vichy nor is it the *Guerra
Sucia*. So much fuss made over the small details. The
books will claim all of it. And there will she remain
at the foot of the pyramid with blood running from
her forehead. Who are fascism's exiles? For now
the prisoners are being dispersed throughout the
country. Their names will be changed before they are
redistributed. Gerda Taro will die in Spain taking
photographs. It will be two decades more before
Robert Capa achieves the same end in Indochina.
So, we have our falling soldiers, each and every one.
And the truth remains uncorroborated. As long as
the academies continue to carry out their selections,
we can continue with our work.

But where have they gone? The public squares were once replete with them. Now they idle in front of their television sets. The New Architecture did not anticipate the emptying of the streets.

We have made ourselves manifest. Now, there is no one left to see.

Feder delivers the first blow. The ribbon is stuck. And the letter *e* has been torn clear from the typewriter.

What year is this?

There are no years anymore. Just this sunken age. And Feder rises steadily with it. Out of the muck. He has much to be proud of. And much to fear, though he may not know it.

The march of time does not concern him. He dreams heavy footsteps, thick boots, long distances, and fine paper wrappers.

But Feder does not dream any more than his sleep resembles sleeping. When he reaches the top stair, he always checks for his glasses before opening the door. The door opens in. This is the only certainty. After, it is up to him. Whatever he does, he is incapable of looking back.

There is a medieval city in the northeast of England of charred stone. The walls like the cobbles underfoot. And no roads in or out. At the edge of the Atlantic it is the same inscrutable church. I pounded my fist against the shore and still the horizon divided nothing, such that the sky plummeted the sea and we were all of us flooded, our bodies strewn there indiscriminately. The canons gutted the beach. None were able to speak. The voices instead crested the waves and dissipated at our feet. Did you scream, Mother? But mother was everyone, the man who held her before defiling me.

The knock on the door startles them. They are guilty of nothing, standing stock still, chisels in hand, like lovers in hiding. But lovers are always, are they not, guilty of something. Simply, they are looking for something, and they want to think they will find it in the fine mesh of the body's bone.

Permission has not been granted for such excavations. But they are losing time. Visibly, the body is beginning to dust itself. The bone is their last chance for meaning.

Fancy that.

Will it?

The door slowly grinds on its hinge.

We ran. We ran faster than anyone had run. And still they caught up with us. Over the wall, past the guards and into the unstable fields. We were scraping ourselves over the earth, scattering our flesh on the scrub, wounding the soil.

Hold on.

When it ended we saw that we were the only ones left. We buried ourselves right there, alive, so to speak, in the shallow earth just before it hardens. When the crows came, we could only appeal to them to go quickly, and spare us the rest of the story.

Dies irae

When the word alluvial enters Feder's mind, he is standing somewhere between his desk and the wall, with the door ajar. A breeze rustles papers, though no window is open and the mechanical bird is knocking its beak against a wooden sill. He shoves his hands into his pockets and notes an absence of feeling then dismisses it at once. The meeting will soon begin. They are all assembled now, waiting most likely for him to arrive with his clipboard and a pencil behind his ear.

Very far from there a new flood-plain claims thousands of dwellings. A small dog manages to free itself from its chain, dragging a post all the way to the edge of town. None of this would have happened had the world been properly calibrated. But Feder cannot have his fingers in everything. Already, a virus is consuming his body's organs, replacing his tissue with a substance resembling charcoal. For now, his blood is forging new channels, but it can't go on like this forever, can it?

Of course not, Feder. Don't trouble yourself with such nonsense. You have four days to make it right.

But he doesn't hear. He has collapsed to the floor with a heavy thud. A fine dust trickles from his ears.

A small dog is lapping it up.

Seldom does Feder remember that he is a man. That he is capable of doing harm.

Did anyone see?

Thunder strikes a blue sky.

A man lies on a square of grass in a quiet part of the city. He turns under the sheet, growls, then hisses, before burrowing his face in the dirt.

They are sweeping up now. A growing pile of leaves mixed with viscera collects at the foot of the stair. Someone has most certainly put his foot in it.

The projectionist has fallen asleep. The screen is a white rectangle of light, illuminating the horror on the faces of the people.

When they tore the sound from my mouth, my eyes went on seeing. It was louder and louder, an intensification of sight at the limit of meaning. The feeling left my extremities, beginning with my fingers, and converging upward, at the neck, until the totality of pain in my body was concentrated there, a small, implacable stone set in my skeleton.

Who would cry in such a place? I did not cry, I wept! And the street cleaners plodded past. And the streets collapsed one into another, a massive garbage heap of streets, with the sounds of creatures trampled underfoot. And nothing was visibly changed.

It was morning. And there was no one about. I saw nothing of what I could have seen.

They put me on trial for trivialities. I died of thirst, and loneliness.

This is the form the pardon took.

We corrected ourselves.

If one were to cut Feder in half, saw him down the middle, say, or chop him up with an axe, one would find much the same studious consistency on the inside as on the outside. He himself, at the limit of his own imagination, once conducted an experiment whereby he turned himself inside out. The persistent illusion was that nothing had changed. Of course, this ability, which might, for some, take the form of a subterfuge, was indicative of the most stalwart normalcy. If Feder has not ever asked the question of heights, it is because he does not consider himself capable of falling. Such that when he hit the ground, his senses were already adjusted to the dissident perspective afforded by the floor. Open or closed, his eyes saw as they had always done. His myopia was of a great service. And the first reason, perhaps, for his having been convoked to this particular post. Every day he walked past the same corpse. Whether or not he could see it, whether or not it was there. What began as a great advantage turned into a great disadvantage, and his manipulations were more and more intimately bound to the spaces through which he moved. These were, of course, reduced to the limited number of footsteps allowed him by the architecture. But it is best not to speak of architecture in such cases. Where Feder went was already accounted for, in that it issued from his own movement. Ultimately, he was responsible for his own death. As to whether or not it would be recorded as a murder, who would be willing to assume such a delicate decision? Regimes are created for such moments of consternation. The question, if it is indeed a question, is disposed of with the body. Remember that the mail chute is interchangeable with the incinerator chute. The principle is the same. If we carried his body this far, it is only out of a concern for distances. That he walked himself here is evidence of a modest success.

We will, however, leave aside the third metamorphosis, caused *accidentally* and from without (especially by insects). It could divert us from the simple path we have to follow, and confuse our purpose. Opportunity may arise elsewhere to speak of these monstrous but rather limited excrescences.

Johann Wolfgang von Goethe

III

THE DECISION

Feder is hanged at dawn.

It is not that I want it but that it wants me.

Increasingly the thought of this clarifies into an action.

TOPOGRAPHY OF A BIRD

The intensity of the energetics of birds and mammals derives from their commitment to maintaining a constant body temperature by the internal generation of heat, which requires high rates of energy acquisition.

Brian K. McNab

I don't want to be moved.

Iannis Xenakis

He closes the door softly behind him, and is heard to say *Oh there you are*. But this is not really what he says. What he says is swallowed back into his mouth, driven into his stomach and forced out the other end of his body, dislocating the coccyx. The last sighs associated with the words run down his legs, leaving behind a strong scent, and the dogs of the city wake in the night to the impudent odour. A few isolated gunshots sound, but it is the screams, foremost, that go unheard, the screams of the people as they are falling asleep. When they wake, the city will scream back at them. For now, there is the thought of the steam ship, a seventy-five day traversal of the seas between hemispheres, a cholera epidemic, and a small bird that nests in leaves. In the early part of the other century, a poet changes his name, but this does nothing to prevent him from being poisoned some seven decades hence by fascist forces convinced of the philanthropic necessity of such actions. A dancer breaks her spine across a length of pipe then dances out her dismemberment. The event is unmemorable, despite having been recorded on tape. One spectator is still cursing himself for having dropped his glasses, since the performance cannot be repeated. All this time, the photographer in the desert is recording the ambivalent apertures of a house of sand. Eventually, he will climb a mountain and never come down from it. The world ocean is a lonely sea. In the midst of the last century, when the hammer falls, two things happen, at least. In the first instance, it strikes a watch. This action is repeated in prefectures distributed across a small country with indifferent boundaries. The watch is removed from the offending wrist and smashed with a hammer, then tossed in a pile with other similarly smashed watches. The other hammer strikes a coffin referred to as a wooden cube. The eighty-four page score accounts for this measure with a single line, reminiscent perhaps of a horizon, or a trip-wire, sometimes a catch is visible, it crackles with the conviction of an extinguished television set spitting out its last electricity. The news says nothing, at the turn of the other century, of the gull eggs doused with formalin, a sterilization procedure employed in a coastal city on rooftop nests, and the sorrow that comes of it; as for the lambs, their limbs are broken by human hands in order to fit them into chicken cages on the way to the Pasqual abattoirs. *May I have this dance?* The continent is careless. The brown speckled gull is trying to sleep. Sterne has a look of permanent consternation on his face. The writer is incapable of distinguishing between justice and freedom. The goats climb into the trees of the coastal region among the modest opiate harvests. It was a crafty cartographer who put Barcelona on a map of Morocco. And drew water from the wells of Paris. *Drinks, anyone?* We urinated on cars and in crevices in the sidewalk. Beating on open doors with our fists. Is this a confession? Name me a poet who isn't an assassin. Show me rain that doesn't carry the plague. The bubonic hour is reserved for everyone. It is a vast hall and the people in it are elegantly dressed. Too elegant to be trusted. Anders comes running through the service door, his tails flapping. Sterne comes running after him. He dies an exasperated death, over and over again. Looking out over mountains, sinking into quicksand, blighted by mosquitoes, and the worms in his intestines. Fornicating, they are fornicating. In the vestiges of flesh, the knife stabs and lethal injections. Put on your nightshirt, it's cold, and here are some slippers for your feet. Anders can name each of the stars in either of the hemispheres. No one will speak to him again. When he stops to catch his breath, he is standing in an open field of tall, yellow grasses. An empty auditorium in the south-west of the old city. And if he has a voice, it is swallowed into the language which has no word for vacuum. He has never seen an albatross, or a leopard. Once he kissed the mouth of a small animal. The autopsy is misleading. Plastics, and small perforations, the teeth, perhaps of a predator, or a metal instrument not designed for killing. He carries a body up a hill. He is beaten with a rope. The tractors comb the sands at the edge of a fresh-water sea. The pier is as old as the century, with its rusted lighthouse at the promontory. *Promise me please.* A list of grievances is drawn, paper napkins are coiled into holders, while extravagant floral arrangements are pushed into blocks of painted polystyrene, each with its germ. Imagine a murder for each of your enemies, and then one each for your friends. I haven't flowered in all the years since I was planted. You say rock bottom but you can't even picture it. The nitrate catches fire as surely as you breathe. So find yourself a sun and burn it. I miss the barricades. The violent confrontations. The identification of the species. Virgin, truant. Who detested whom. The terns with their orange beaks; the birds that fall with their nests onto the rocks. Murder. The civilization owed everything to a single word. Anders is lying on Sterne's back. He turns him over. They run past churches and climb onto trams, through sewers and over rooftops, leaping from ship decks onto docks, and balancing in the air between buildings, the sands of deserts in their mouths, swinging from chandeliers. Neither has heard of Jean Sénac, or Euripides, or the name of the new disease. Their elegance is owed in part to the purple flush of their faces. In other languages they speak of taking their leave. The song of the hermit thrush is fine bone and night. The sandpiper is water and salt and solitude. In the museum of executed bodies, the glass cases are all empty, their contents having spilled onto the floor. It rains into the mouths of handsome dictators, caracolling past wheat fields on horse carcasses in winter. None of this is invention. It's all made up. In the manner of the politicians and the landed gentry. Slipping ten-pound notes into an old man's panty. He takes an oblique view of history and cocks his gun. One such hunter counted forty, forty flocks fallen from forty skies. And the roar of admiring crowds. They are hanged by their feet with their skirts up. When it rains it doesn't stop. There are obscenity trials for near misses. And treason to grist the Ferris wheels. And plush carpets and fine sherry and shooting galleries and false bottoms and depleted uranium. The house is grand and it is lit from the field. Visible from the sea, and across the street. *Tell me Sterne, what you've never told anyone. I'll walk you all the way there under cover of night. Listen for me.* The search-lights will illuminate the undiscovered bodies, buried or burned, twisted around banisters, mounted on spires or weathervanes. She misses every bit of it. The awards ceremony and the decorative cowhides, the movement of objects and the camera trained away from obvious sight lines. Anders leans over Sterne just as Sterne leans over Anders. Always with a sense of precipice, and numbers. A steep hill and a wooden shack. A mountain and a magistrate. *Wake up!* There is a pistol or there is an earthquake. It is an unremarkable morning after a night of revelry. The coffee burns and the flowers lose their petals, and these are just banalities. No one but Sterne running from Anders or Anders leading Sterne away; there are two such cast-offs in the middle of the new continent, clothed or unclothed, under the gaslights, with passports each assigned to different names. We swore under our breath, we swore we'd leave the country. I was my enemy's own enemy. *There is a cemetery in an oil field and a wall over which I pass. I leave a finger to the wire barbs and a limb to the minera, and this bit of skin.* There is such a flag as flies over the murdered cities. There is such a one as vouches for the combine. The voice raked over coal mines and fantasticated skies. Rasping, rasping. *Sorry I'm late.* We waited all afternoon. We were held up. At arm's length and into the perverted bestiaries. What is there to envy? Someone shakes the door at night, shakes it violently from its post. Sterne was shattered glass, didn't I tell you? And Anders was his obituary. You could call it truth, with all of history's capitals. A bedrock given to the elements, a failed epistolary, a finely tuned explosive, an ice machine. Look inside the prison cell in the last block, past the guards to where the floor graduates. They are embracing now. You know what happens next. Do you hear the church bells with their countdown? That's somebody's head. Remember the eel hunters with their wet suits and headlamps and their feet bare in the black sand. The stars are all dead already. Harpooned in someone's sleep. We are carbon deposits, making records of things. *What did you think?* Along the shores of all the lakes and all the seas armies of ordinary humans flush the creatures out. You can hear them in the leaves. Footsteps soft as dirt. They come at them from all sides.

What did I give of myself that I could have given to another?

The body is dropped at Argentina's feet. It is wrapped in algae, shoals of fish, caked with plankton, salt specked, skin flecks, coral broken against the teeth.

Release the shutter once, and everything comes to an end.

Nakahira Takuma

TABLE OF VALUES

There exists no recording of the Austrian philosopher's voice. If he refused to give it to the tape deck, if he deliberately bequeathed it to oblivion, in the century of technology, of ferry boats and unguents, propellers and sliding doors, he nonetheless confided his face to the photo booth. For if the photograph, according to a renowned mathematician, is a controlled chemical catastrophe, the precision of its structure by language would entail certain destruction. The image is a form of consternation, oblivion is its necessary vocation, the inscription of its defeat, of a certain recognition. A flutter. Not unspeakable, but unspoken.

—Nathanaël
2011-2014

Intertitle. "The living themselves" is language grafted from *Between Past and Future* by Hannah Arendt.

31. Italicised text: Iannis Xenakis. 32. Italicised text: Hannah Arendt.

Fingerprint on front cover is owed to Francis Galton's experiments.

Epigraph translations are by G.E.M. Anscombe, P.M.S. Hacker and Joachim Schulte (Wittgenstein), Nathanaël (Didi-Huberman), Derek Yeld (Xenakis), Edmund Jephcott (Benjamin), Douglas Miller (Goethe), Imamura Takaya and Ivan Vartanian (Nakahira).

The author is indebted to Stephen Motika and to Nathaniel Feis for their steadfast solidarity and accompaniment. And to Kit Schluter for such fine tracings.

ISBN: 978-1-937658-56-4

Design and typesetting by Kit Schluter

Text set in Adobe Jenson Pro and a modified University Roman

Cataloging-in-publication data is available
from the Library of Congress

Distributed by the University Press of New England
One Court Street
Lebanon, NH 03766
www.upne.com

Nightboat Books
New York
www.nightboat.org

The following individuals have supported the publication of this
book. We thank them for their generosity and commitment to the
mission of Nightboat Books:

Elizabeth Motika
Benjamin Taylor

In addition, this book has been made possible, in part, by a grant
from the National Endowment for the Arts and the New York
State Council on the Arts Literature Program.